Dina Island

Honey McGregor

Honey McGregor

Visit my website at www.honeymcgregor.blogspot.com

Published by Honey McGregor
Also by Honey McGregor
Private Pleasures: The Collection
Watch Me Want Me

Table of Contents

The Arrival

Racquel felt a rush of anxiety swoop through her body as she alighted from the small aircraft. What was she doing here? She thought back to the many times she and Martin had stepped off a plane at the beginning of a trip, filled with excitement at the adventures ahead of them. They'd had great times together, it was so unfair that their future together had been stolen from them so brutally.

'Mrs Hampton?' a voice enquired, interrupting her scrambled thoughts. She looked up to see a man standing in front of her, smartly dressed, wearing a chauffeur's cap. She nodded affirmatively and allowed the chauffeur to take her bag.

'Welcome to Dina Island, I'm Georges, please come with me, your suitcase is already in the vehicle.' He turned and led the way to a waiting jeep, opening the door and stepping aside to allow her to climb in.

Well, there was certainly no going back so she may as well embrace it and try to enjoy herself.

Settling back in the jeep she allowed her thoughts to wander as Georges silently drove them to her destination.

It had been her best friend Stella's idea, 'You'll love it honey, trust me, it's just what you need. You haven't had a vacation since you lost Martin, it's been three years darling and you're too young to be hiding away scared of life. I've checked it all out, read the reviews, it's totally above board and absolutely private, exactly what you've been talking about. You have to apply though, it's terribly exclusive, I've heard of some women not being accepted no matter how many different dates they suggested. But I'm sure you'll be fine, you're flexible with dates and you're totally deserving of a rejuvenating vacation.'

It was true, she thought, looking out of the window at the passing scenery of palm trees, sandy beaches and blue sea, she had said more than once that she would love to get away somewhere beautiful. 'Somewhere private,' she had mused to Stella, 'where she could relax, feel pampered, have a vacation but without the people.' She had thought it an impossible ask but Stella had made it her mission in life to find her the perfect package. Having gone to so much effort Racquel had thought that she could hardly let her friend down by refusing to go. It was very expensive, horrendously so, clearly only for the very wealthy, but Martin had left her extremely well provided for so there was really no reason not to follow through.

The jeep silently rolled to a halt at the end of a sandy lane and Racquel couldn't help smiling with delight at the scene in front of her. A pretty villa sat in a clearing, surrounded by gently swaying palm trees and she could see a path leading around the side to a little beach.

'This, Mrs Hampton, is your home for the next week,' Georges turned around, smiling, before getting out of the jeep and opening her door. 'Mr Baron, your host, will be along later to welcome you, but in the meantime, settle in and make yourself at home.' He led the way, carrying her bags, and opened the door, stepping back for her to enter ahead of him.

Racquel walked into the villa, noting appreciatively the beautiful, but simple, décor. The floors were of burnished cement screed with a scattering of sisal rugs, the walls painted in natural shades to reflect the light. Occasional tables were dotted around, topped with wooden sculptures and lamps and a luxurious looking lounge suite upholstered in ivory, with an assortment of cushions, was set in the lounge area, with French doors open to a patio, overlooking the small beach. A coffee table in the lounge was loaded with magazines, books and an overflowing bowl of fruit, together with a beautiful arrangement of red roses, and she could see a door leading off to the bedroom.

Georges had placed her bags in the bedroom and returned now, saying goodbye and that he hoped she enjoyed her time at Villa Tali. What a beautiful name, she thought, already feeling relaxation seep through her body.

She walked out onto the patio and gazed at the ocean ahead of her. It was almost totally calm, the water just gently lapping onto the white sand. Stella had been right, this was what she needed! She walked back inside and entered the bedroom, a calm space of natural hues, large potted palms in the corners and a huge bed taking centre stage. Laying on top of the white lace-edged duvet was a folder and Racquel picked it up.

Quality ivory coloured card encased thick sheets of paper, the whole package bound with a cream, silk, ribbon through its centre. A simple gold logo of a palm tree and the name 'Tali' graced the front of the folder and inside she read the simple welcome message:

Welcome to Villa Tali, Mrs Hampton. We hope that your experience is everything that you have wished for. We wish you days and nights of relaxation, pleasure and re-awakening.

She smiled to herself, yes, that was exactly what she was hoping for! Turning the page, she read on, noting that her host was Mr Baron and that he would be dropping in to welcome her at 3pm. Checking her watch she saw that she had a couple of hours to unpack and settle in, time too for a shower and a change of clothes...

A beautiful broderie anglaise robe hung on a clothes hanger in the bathroom and, after finishing off her luxurious shower with a generous application of the silken body lotion she had found in the basket of toiletries, she slipped it on and unpacked her suitcase.

Upon opening the wardrobe Racquel was surprised to find a number of pieces of clothing hanging in the closet. Looking at the labels she realised that they were all her size. A memory came back to her. When she had completed the website questionnaire, she had been asked all manner of rather strange questions such as her clothing size, shoe size, beverages of choice, foods of choice, favourite authors, movies too, and even if she enjoyed any recreational drugs!

Hanging her clothes on the spare hangers, she looked around for somewhere to place her folded items and underwear. She spied a pretty, baroque cabinet with drawers, perfect.

Again, when she opened the top drawer, there were already some items folded inside. A beautiful bikini, white with little gold flowers printed on the fabric, some denim shorts, tees and, in the second drawer, a selection of lingerie. Picking up one of the lace bras she checked its size, yes, it would fit her perfectly, this was way beyond her expectations but what a pleasure!

She finished putting her own clothing away and wandered through to the lounge. The sight of the delicious fruits in their bowl reminded her that she was a little hungry and she picked up a ripe peach, sinking her teeth into its sweetness, its juices running down her chin. A feeling of unexpected happiness flowed through her and she wandered out to the little patio to finish her fruit while enjoying the perfect view.

Checking her watch a few minutes later Racquel decided that she should dress in preparation for her host's arrival. She really didn't feel like seeing anyone, let alone talking to anyone, but she guessed that this was just a courtesy call and that she would then be left alone in absolute privacy, as per her request on the website form.

But what to wear? She had packed pretty basic clothing for her trip, planning to just rest, lie around reading, and swim in the warm ocean when the fancy took her. The sight of the beautiful selection of clothing hanging in the closet, however, caused her to hesitate, maybe she should try something on...

Her fingers flipped through the hangers, a short, sheer kaftan with little pearl buttons running down its front, a long floral sundress with pintucking to the bodice, a short black dress with shoestring straps and a large bow to the bust, a white halter neck... she paused, took it off the hanger, yes...

Slipping the halter neck dress over her head she realised that she wasn't wearing any underwear, and then observed that a bra would not be necessary. She was not naturally full breasted and the dress did not suit a bra anyway. Panties, however, would be necessary, and so, turning to the chest of drawers, she selected a pair of panties. Her plain selection of functional undergarments suddenly seemed too bland and her fingers reached for one of the items placed there for her to wear. The little white lace thong fitted beautifully (of course) and she let the dress drop down over it, where it settled just above her knees.

Feeling suddenly quite girlish and light-hearted she reached for her flip flops and then wondered if footwear had also been provided somewhere. Looking around she noticed a slim cupboard in the corner of the room and, upon opening it, found it stocked with a wonderful assortment of sandals. It was every girl's dream! What girl wouldn't melt at the sight of shelves of beautiful footwear, all in her size, just for her!

She slipped her feet into a pair of nude, wedge, mules and twirled in front of the full length mirror. This was fun! But silly! She was, after all, vacationing on her own, what was she doing getting all dressed up? Maybe it was for the mysterious Mr Baron... She shook her head and smiled, he was just the travel company's host, doing his job, welcoming her and then, presumably leaving her alone to enjoy her relaxing vacation.

Still, as she was feeling in a happy mood, she decided to apply a little make-up and spritz on some perfume.

She should have realised that there would be a selection of perfume too, she mused, as she opened the bathroom cabinet and found an array of glass bottles. Ah, Chanel Cristalle, that took her back to her younger days. Memories of hot summer's days flooded her head, going out on dates, the anticipation of the evening ahead, the scent of fresh, light, youthfulness... she could actually smell it...

As Racquel realised that she had automatically spritzed the Cristalle onto her neck and wrists there was a gentle humming sound of a doorbell. It must be Mr Baron, he was right on time.

She walked to the door and opened it, smiling in welcome as her host appeared before her.

Mr Baron

'Mrs Hampton, I'm Mr Baron, it's a pleasure to meet you,' said the Adonis standing before her.

Raquel did a double take. She had been expecting, for some unknown reason, an older man, dressed, perhaps, in a shirt and pants, business like. This man could not have been further from her imaginations. He was tall and sun tanned, with longish, fair hair tied back in a pony tail. He was wearing denim cut-offs, frayed at the bottoms, revealing firm, muscular, legs, and a partially buttoned shirt revealed an equally firm chest, adorned with a simple cowrie shell on a leather thong around his neck. Bare feet completed his outfit but it was his looks which took Racquel's breath away. His blue eyes smiled into hers and his mouth curled up at the corners in the most attractive way. He must be about her age too, mid-thirties...

Mr Baron extended his hand towards Racquel and she took it, aware of how firm his handshake was. He was wearing a number of leather thongs around his wrists and she breathed in a sudden scent of his aftershave, fresh and manly. All in all, a very attractive package...

Racquel smiled, 'Lovely to meet you, please come in, this place is beautiful!' Turning, she led the way to the lounge, then paused, not sure what to do next.

Mr Baron took the lead, 'Nelson Mandela once said: *The English have given us many things including brandy. But afternoon tea, that is the greatest*,' and, gently taking hold of her arm, he steered her out to the patio.

Racquel gave a little gasp. A small table had appeared and was laid with a crisp, white, linen cloth, with, in its centre, a tiered cake stand loaded with delicious goodies taking pride of place. The whole ensemble was finished off with a white tea pot, cups and saucers, and, finally tea plates topped with flower adorned, folded, napkins. 'When did you? How did you?' Racquel looked at him in astonishment.

Mr Baron smiled enigmatically, 'We have our ways... and a little bird told me that you happen to enjoy the finer things in life, particularly a luxurious afternoon tea!'

Of course, thought Racquel, the website again, all the details she had filled in, her likes and dislikes, her pleasures, favourite pastimes, even her taste in men.... which, come to think of it, matched almost perfectly Mr Baron's exceedingly good looks...

As Mr Baron held her seat out for her, Racquel thanked him and sat down, crossing her legs and admiring her painted nails in the pretty nude mules, pleased that she had taken her friend Stella's advice to have a pedicure as part of her preparation for her trip.

'I hope you've settled in alright? asked Mr Baron as he expertly poured the tea through the strainer placed on the cup, 'milk?' Racquel nodded and took a sip of her tea before replying.

'I have, thank you,' she smiled, 'it really wasn't difficult, everything is so perfect, I feel so relaxed already.'

'Well that is exactly what we strive for,' grinned Mr Baron, 'now, eat, you must be hungry!'

She was, and picking up her plate, she selected a couple of delicate finger sandwiches, biting into one and savouring the taste of the cream cheese and cucumber. So traditional, so perfect.

The couple munched companionably for a few minutes and, when Racquel had touched the napkin to her lips after indulging in a final cream laden scone, she sighed. 'That really was too delicious Mr Baron, I couldn't have imagined a more perfect welcome, thank you!'

'I'd like you to call me Anthony, if you're comfortable with that,' he paused, looking at her enquiringly.

'And please call me Racquel,' she realised that she felt very comfortable with him and wondered how much she would see of him during her time on Dina.

'I certainly will, Racquel, thank you,' his smile touched his eyes and they glinted slightly, a promise of fun to be enjoyed, if she so wished.

They chatted for a while and Anthony explained a few things, although most of it was in her folder, which she had glanced through earlier. Then, standing up, Anthony informed her that he would be leaving her in peace, to relax and enjoy her villa and private beach.

Racquel felt a stab of disappointment, realising that she didn't really want him to leave her, at least not just yet. 'Must you go already?' she asked, not wanting to appear needy but hoping that she could change his mind.

Anthony grinned, 'well, if you want to put up with me a little longer, how about some champagne then?' With that he gently clapped his hands and a young woman appeared, as if from nowhere. 'This is Nobu, she will be taking care of you, discreetly, and preparing all your meals.'

Racquel and Nobu smiled at one another and Racquel said that if the tea she had just enjoyed so much was an example of the kind of care she could expect from Nobu then she thought she was going to be very happy and very spoilt.

Nobu expertly wheeled the little table away and returned with a bottle of Moet & Chandon in an ice bucket, two champagne glasses balanced in the top. This she placed on the small bistro table beside them before quietly disappearing again.

'My favourite!' exclaimed Racquel, before grinning foolishly and looking at Anthony, 'Of course! I should be getting the hang of this by now, all the questions on the form I filled in, it's all making sense.'

Anthony took one of Racquel's hands in his, a little jolt of excitement running through her as he did so, 'Racquel, your whole time here has been planned to give you exactly what you were looking for, and what we felt you needed, we take our job very seriously.'

Our job, of course, he was just doing his job, she must remember that, he was not there for her pleasure, or his own, she had expressly noted that she did not want to spend time in anyone's company. And yet... now that she was here... she was feeling so, different... she felt more alive than she had for years. She realised that she wouldn't mind spending time in Anthony's company at all. But he was working, she was just his client... but what was that he was saying?

'You know that you can change your wishes at any time? If you feel that you would like some company, anything else at all, you have only to let me know. I assure you it will not be a hardship to spend time in the company of such a beautiful woman...' He was looking intently into her eyes, still holding her hand, and she felt her spirits lift.

'I feel so different already,' she wanted to explain, 'I thought I wouldn't be able to cope with other people, I haven't had a vacation since I lost my husband...' Anthony nodded understandingly, (he was, of course, aware of what had happened to Martin, it was all in the form) 'but I find that I am enjoying this afternoon with you more than I've enjoyed anything for a long time.' She blushed, wondering if she was saying too much.

He smiled gently, 'I'm very pleased to hear you say that, I'm enjoying myself tremendously too, more than I should perhaps...' He gently released her hand and expertly eased the cork from the bottle before pouring them both some Moet. They clinked glasses. 'To you, Racquel.' She responded, 'To you, Anthony, and Dina, thank you.'

Sipping their champagne, she wondered what her evening had planned for her. She supposed Nobu would be taking care of her evening meal plans and wondered what Anthony did during his evenings on the island. Then a thought struck her, maybe he didn't even stay on the island?

As if reading her thoughts Anthony spoke. 'I stay on the island, just around the other side, it's a very small island, only about ten kilometres long. I am on hand if you need me, any time, for anything. You can just raise the little flag over there.' She looked in the direction he was pointing and saw a little pole with a white flag. 'And I mean *anything*, Racquel,' he was looking into her eyes intently and she felt a stirring inside her.

7

'I might just take you up on that,' she grinned, feeling suddenly rather flirtatious, and was pleased when he responded with a grin, saying that he hoped she did so.

The champagne finished she realised that Anthony was probably going to leave her now and wished that he was staying for the evening ahead.

Again, as if reading her thoughts, he said that he must be going and that he hoped she enjoyed her evening meal and that she slept well.

Disappointment rushed through her but she smiled and thanked him, before walking with him to the door and watching him drive off in a golf cart with a final wave of his hand.

She wandered disconsolately back inside. What was wrong with her? Wasn't this what she wanted? Time alone?

The Gift

Her eyes alighted on a gift-wrapped package on the table in the lounge. That had not been there earlier, how odd! It was quite large and she picked it up, noticing a small card attached to the outside.

If you change your mind and feel like some company this evening, I think you'll find this will fit you perfectly. I'd be delighted to join you for dinner at 7pm. Just raise the flag,(but no pressure) Anthony.

Taking the package through to the bedroom, Racquel unwrapped it in anticipation, gasping in delight as she lifted out its contents.

A beautiful dress in soft, pale gold silk, shimmered and slipped through her fingers onto the bed, a filmy, nude, wisp of lace dropping on top of it. Picking it up she realised that it was a thong, then, noticing that the box contained further items, she lifted out the delicate, also nude, strappy sandals, placing them on the bed beside the beautiful outfit.

There remained a little suede pouch in the bottom of the box and she pulled its drawstrings apart to reveal a twisted white gold chain holding a large, burnished stone pendant. It was beautiful, selected to perfectly compliment the outfit.

Racquel made her decision, she *would* invite Anthony to join her for dinner! Feeling excited, and a little foolish, she walked out to the flagpole and raised the little white flag. Then a thought occurred to her, how would Nobu know that dinner would be for two and not one? Looking around, she saw a movement inside and Nobu came through to the patio, table linen in her arms.

'Er, Nobu, I will be having company for dinner this evening, I hope that's not a problem?'

Nobu smiled, reassuring her, and proceeded to lay the table, placing two sets of cutlery down as she did so.

Racquel had a strange feeling, it was as if her every thought was anticipated. It was not an unpleasant feeling, rather a complete relinquishing of all responsibility and decision making.

She left Nobu busy on the patio and went back through to the bedroom, breathing in the delicious cooking smells emanating from the small kitchen, as she passed by.

Lifting her white dress off over her head, she slipped the gorgeous, gold, silk sheath on in its place, her skin responding to its touch with a slight shiver of pleasure. It fell to calf length and fitted her body snugly. Slipping off her white panties she replaced them with the nude lace, again allowing the dress to shimmer and slide its way back down to her calves.

An image came unbidden into her head, of Anthony's hands lifting the dress slowly up to reveal the nude lace, then further, to reveal her small breasts, and she felt a little tug between her legs. God, she was getting carried away! She was behaving like a teenager on a date! Nonetheless, no matter what she told herself, there was no doubt that she was attracted to him and excited about the evening ahead.

She finished off her outfit with the delicate sandals and hung the chain around her neck, the heavy pendant resting just between her breasts, pulling the silky fabric tight and revealing the hardness of her nipples beneath it.

Having fixed up her hair in an elegant knot, Racquel wondered what to do until Anthony arrived. She decided to fix herself a drink and watch the sunset from the patio.

A drinks trolley had been placed on the patio (Nobu thought of everything!) and she fixed a gin and tonic, the perfect sundowner, before reclining on the cushion laden daybed with its perfect view of the ocean and setting sun.

Dreamily she allowed her thoughts to wander... this was paradise, beyond her wildest dreams, she could never have imagined such a beautiful setting... and to be spending the evening with such a handsome man... she couldn't wish for more right now. Stella had truly found her the perfect vacation when she introduced her to www.privateislandescapes.blogspot.com.

In no time she was aware of Anthony's presence, the sound of ice clinking in a glass awakening her from her reverie, and she looked up to see him coming towards her. He was wearing a loosely buttoned white, linen shirt, with khaki linen pants, this time with leather thongs on his feet.

'Thank you for inviting me,' he smiled, as she stood up, also smiling. 'I feel like you're reading my mind,' she said, aware of his eyes taking in her body sheathed in the pale gold silk. 'You knew that I would feel lonely this evening.'

'Sometimes Dina has a special effect on people,' he explained, 'she has a way of changing our minds, opening us to new possibilities. What we think we want is not always what we need.'

Taking her hand, he gently kissed it and Racquel felt her stomach flutter. 'I'm pleased to see how well the outfit fitted, you look stunning, I hope you're wearing all of it?'

Racquel blushed, was he flirting with her? 'It's perfect, like everything else, thank you, and yes, I am wearing all of it.' She grinned, feeling suddenly flirtatious, and why not?

The evening was incredible, Nobu's food, of exceptional quality, was devoured by them both in between much talking and laughing, and they had finished their second bottle of Kistler Chardonnay before enjoying their dessert of miniature white chocolate cheesecakes.

Dina Island

It seemed that Anthony was as keen as she was for the evening to never end, his suggestion of a glass of 21 year Chivas Royal Salute to round off the meal the proof, if any were needed.

She watched him pour the whisky and expertly drop the ice into the heavy glasses, happily moving to the daybed when he suggested it.

Leaning back Racquel realised that his arm was casually draped around the back of the bed, his fingers just brushing the bare skin of her shoulders.

Now that dusk had descended, little twinkling lights had appeared everywhere, discreetly strung around the patio and its surroundings. Racquel sighed in contentment, leaning back a little further and feeling Anthony's arm rest a little more heavily around her shoulders.

'What a perfect evening,' she murmured happily, taking a sip of her whisky.

'Indeed,' he murmured, before gently taking her glass and placing it on the side table, together with his own.

Shifting slightly, Anthony gently cupped her chin with his other hand. 'A perfect evening in the company of the most perfectly beautiful woman, if I may say so.' His lips gently brushed hers as his eyes smouldered into hers and she felt herself melt with weakness.

He kissed her again and she found herself responding hungrily, readily parting her lips as his tongue gently probed her mouth. His free hand gently stroked her bare shoulder and arm before sliding over the silk of her dress, pausing to circle her hard nipples, then gliding down, over her hips and thighs.

Her thoughts were in chaos, she suddenly wanted him madly but it was against everything she'd said she wished her trip to be.

As his lips touched her neck she realised she was powerless to resist and allowed herself to respond willingly, moving closer to him and arching her body into his, her arm snaking around his neck, drawing him closer to her.

Their legs were stretched out together on the daybed and Anthony's hand effortlessly found the hem of her silk shift, sliding it slowly up her legs, just as she had imagined earlier.

He paused, pulling away from her, 'Are you ok with this?' She nodded, not wanting him to stop, and he pulled her firmly against him as his free hand slid her dress further, to reveal her lacy thong.

He slipped his fingers inside the lace and her wetness flooded over them at his touch, her gasps the only sound in the silence of the evening.

Anthony kissed her again before shifting his body lower down the daybed, his mouth seeking out her hot, inviting, wetness. She arched towards him, wanting his tongue inside her and he didn't disappoint, expertly licking, sucking and probing her until she felt the first waves of her orgasm flood through her. She groaned with sheer pleasure and pushed herself harder against his mouth until her body quietened.

11

He moved back up to lay beside her on the cushions, gently pulling her dress back down to cover her, and held her in his arms.

'How was that for your first evening on Dina, Racquel?' he enquired with a teasing smile.

'Unexpected and totally amazing,' she smiled into his eyes, 'but what about you?'

'Your pleasure is my pleasure, and it really was my pleasure,' he replied enigmatically.

He took her hand and guided her from the daybed as he stood up. 'It's time for me to say goodnight my beautiful Racquel.'

She felt a little stab of disappointment, realising that she wished he was staying the night so that they could continue their lovemaking.

Not wanting to show her feelings so openly she smiled at him, and thanked him for a special evening, as they walked to the door of the villa.

With a kiss goodbye he was gone, leaving her feeling confused and wanting so much more.

She closed the door and, not sure what to do next, decided to pour herself another whisky and take a few moments to calm down on the daybed.

As she sipped her whisky, she found herself reliving their earlier moments and was surprised at how horny she still felt. She allowed her hand to touch herself through the silk of her dress, imagining it was his hand, first touching her nipples until they stood hard and erect through the fabric, then moving down to gently touch herself where his mouth had teased her to orgasm earlier.

She felt herself getting wet again instantly and pulled her dress up to expose the lace thong. Still imagining it was his fingers, she slipped her own fingers inside the lace to touch herself, her fingers gliding easily over her swollen clit. Impatiently she pulled her dress off, exposing her nakedness, although there was no-one to see it but herself. She allowed her other hand to caress her nipples as she imagined his mouth on her.

As she was about to come she plunged her fingers inside herself, imagining they were his cock, and, moving them in and out, she moaned out loud as she climaxed for the second time that evening.

Sitting at his desk, Anthony grasped his erect cock and moved his hand faster and faster up and down the length of his shaft, his eyes glued to the monitor in front of him. As Racquel brought herself to orgasm he came too, his cum spilling onto his leg, and he fell back with a gasp, hearing her moan as she also fell back amongst the cushions of the day bed.

He smiled to himself, she was perfect, in every way. He looked forward to exploring that beautiful body further, especially now that she had so thoughtfully provided him with a sneak preview of the whole package. Then he frowned slightly, her sheer perfection had carried him away somewhat though, he'd never made a move on one of his guests on the first night before. Still, she'd definitely enjoyed it, and he hadn't frightened her off at all, so it should all be fine...

Racquel looked around self consciously, silly, there was no-one to see her, and yet she had the strangest feeling, as if she was being observed...

Picking up her dress she made her way through to the bedroom and, within a few minutes, slipped off to a deep sleep in between the cool sheets.

Honey McGregor

The Private Beach

Upon waking the next morning Racquel found her thoughts drifting back to the previous evening. What an unexpected turn of events! She wondered when she would next see Anthony, would he call in, or would he wait for her to make the next move? Perhaps she should raise the white flag, which, come to think of it, was a little like surrendering. How perfect, she *did* want to surrender, to her desires, to *him*!

It was a beautiful, hot, day and, after a quick shower she slipped the white bikini on, pulling on the little denim shorts over the bottoms. Wandering barefoot through to the lounge she saw that Nobu had opened up the doors and laid her a breakfast table on the patio.

A glass dish was filled with layers of rich, Greek yoghurt, small pieces of fruit and granola and, after drizzling some honey over it she ate hungrily while looking at the calm water gently lapping at the sand. Nobu appeared quietly and offered her coffee and eggs, to which she acquiesced happily. She could get used to this lifestyle!

Having breakfasted to her fill, she left the patio and walked the few steps to the beach and the water's edge. The water was so warm, she began to wander along, the water bathing her feet.

A gentle humming sound broke her reverie and she looked around to see what it was.

'Ahoy there!' called a familiar voice and her face broke into a grin as she realised it was Anthony, in a small motor boat, just rounding the rocky point which created her private little cove.

She waved and watched him bring the boat in to a small jetty which she had not noticed the day before.

She walked to meet him, admiring his tanned, bare, upper body, his muscles flexing, as he tied the mooring rope around the wooden pole on the jetty. He was barefoot, like her, and wearing only a pair of frayed denim shorts.

She felt a little self-conscious but he put her at her ease with a hug and a light kiss on her lips, holding her gently by the shoulders and pulling back to enquire how she had slept.

'I slept like a baby,' she informed him, as her stomach fluttered at his embrace.

'I take a little cruise around the island every couple of days to check that everything is fine and I wondered if you'd like to join me. But if you'd rather be alone...'

She shook her head, 'No,' I'd love to, thanks!'

His eyes raked her body in approval. 'I'm pleased to see what a perfect fit the bikini is,' he grinned, 'jump aboard, I have everything that you'll need right here.'

I'll bet you do, thought Racquel, feeling excitement mounting inside her.

They set off and the slight breeze was welcome in the heat. As they slowly cruised along, they chatted and Anthony pointed out small landmarks around the island's coastline. It was quite rocky, with vegetation growing down close to the waterline in places, the odd surprise patch of white sand announcing the presence of a little beach, perfect for sunbathing, and so much more...

After about an hour Anthony dropped anchor and stilled the engine, the boat bobbing in the water and not a soul to be seen. 'How about a swim?' he asked her, taking her hand and helping her up. 'You'll need to take your shorts off... I take it you're wearing both parts of that bikini?'

She unzipped the shorts and slid them down her legs, conscious the whole time that Anthony was watching her from under his hooded lids. Kicking them off she followed him to the little step at the back of the boat.

He stopped and undid his shorts, letting them drop to his feet, before kicking them off and standing there fully naked. She gasped, trying to draw her eyes away from his erect cock, and feeling herself go weak with desire. Am I losing control? thought Anthony. Am I taking this all too fast? But the glint of excitement in her eyes told him that everything was okay, and so he laughed and dropped into the water, turning to watch her as she also dropped in.

The water was like a bath and they bobbed around together until he took her in his arms, kissing her suddenly and fiercely. She responded instantly, their tongues intertwining and he moved his hands over her body as she tentatively began to explore his.

Her hand found his cock and she took hold of it, noticing with pleasure that he let out a small moan. By now he was undoing her bikini top and, as her small breasts escaped their confines, he flung it back onto the boat before lowering his mouth to them.

His firm arms supported her as she wrapped her legs around his thighs, his lips moving over her nipples to kiss and suck them, his tongue flicking them teasingly until she couldn't bear it any longer. She wanted him so much!

Anthony freed one hand to lower her bikini bottom down her legs and over her feet, again throwing it onto the boat, where it teetered precariously on the edge before slowly falling into the water and disappearing. 'Whoops!' smiled Anthony, shrugging and raising his eyebrows.

With both of them fully naked there was nothing to hold them back and they kissed each other hungrily, their hands exploring each other's bodies, their legs gently moving to keep them afloat.

She was so hot for him, she wanted him to fuck her right there and she pressed herself against his hardness to show him that she wanted him inside her. I can't believe I'm doing this, she thought in surprise, I feel so horny.

But Anthony was not to be rushed, he pulled away and smiled into her eyes, 'Let's get back onto the boat,' he whispered.

Lifting one of the seats he took out a large towel and wrapped it around her, before taking one for himself and wrapping it loosely around his hips.

He started the boat's motor again and expertly steered it into the next cove, toward a little private beach, surrounded on all sides by rocks and bushes, a lone palm tree swaying gently in the breeze. Having dropped the anchor, he pulled on his shorts and grabbed a blanket and his phone, shrugging and saying 'In case I'm needed,' apologetically. Racquel slipped her shorts on, conscious of the denim against her nakedness and went to replace her bikini top. 'Leave it,' he whispered, touching her arm.

Holding hands, they stepped into the water and waded the few steps to the sand. Racquel was overcome with an enormous feeling of freedom, from being under the warm sun, and in the cool sea, wearing only a tiny pair of denims and with the most gorgeous man!

Anthony laid out the blanket with a shake of his arm before turning to Racquel and taking her in his arms. He kissed her hard, his mouth grinding against hers, and she responded, pushing her breasts against his chest and wrapping her arms around his neck.

He walked her backwards towards the palm tree until her bare back touched it. 'Stand there,' he whispered, before slowly kissing and caressing her bare breasts and arms, her body, all the way down to where the denim covered her hungry sex.

Her fingers roamed over the bulge in the front of his shorts, playing with the zip and then releasing him so that his shorts dropped and he stood, naked again, his cock proudly sticking out, hard and erect, all for her.

She was wet, so wet, so turned on, all she could think about was his cock and how much she wanted it inside her.

Anthony's hands slowly and agonisingly unzipped her shorts before lowering them down her legs so that she could step out of them. He dropped to his knees in front of her and began to kiss her stomach, her hips, her thighs, his hands all the while caressing her legs. She squirmed in desperation, parting her legs slightly to give him better access to her.

Obligingly his mouth moved towards her straining mound, kissing her and licking her with little flicks of his tongue. With one hand he gently parted the lips of her secret parts, her wetness creaming onto his fingers as his mouth found her.

He began to tease her clit with his tongue, sliding it around and sucking gently as she gasped and pushed harder against him. He sucked harder and pressed his mouth against her as she ground against him, finding her rhythm and moving against him as she came closer to climaxing.

Suddenly she came in a rush, unable to stop, her orgasm cascading out of her as she cried out, her body arching uncontrollably and Anthony continued to suck her until she calmed, finally falling back against the palm tree, sated and weak from the intensity of it all.

He gently took her hand and led her to the blanket, lowering her to the ground and lying beside her, stroking her hair and gazing into her eyes.

She felt for his cock and began to slowly glide her hand up and down along its length as it began to grow even bigger. She was so hungry for him, the throbbing between her legs was so urgent and she pulled him towards her.

Suddenly Anthony looked up, as if he could hear something. 'I'm sorry,' he groaned, 'I must just check my phone,' before reaching for it. Reading the message he frowned, 'How inconvenient, it appears that I'm needed back at the office shortly.' He sighed, 'I'm so sorry, we'll have to head back...'

Racquel felt disappointment flood through her body, she couldn't believe it, a few moments more and he would have been inside her! She tried to hide her feelings by smiling understandingly, saying, 'It's ok, I know you have to work, not all of us are on vacation after all.'

He lifted her up and pulled her into his arms, kissing her gently, before smiling with that little lift of his eyebrows again. 'Thank you,' he whispered, 'for being so understanding.'

The ride back was completed in record time and before Racquel knew it she was back on her own little beach, the only differing factor being that she was minus her bikini bottoms.

Anthony had excused himself, apologising again for having to cut short their excursion and explained that he would be tied up for the rest of the day and evening.

Not wanting to appear desperate, Racquel had reassured him that it was fine, she would enjoy relaxing at her villa, and her heart had lifted when he suggested joining her for dinner the following evening.

She wandered slowly up to her patio, the throbbing between her legs no less urgent than earlier. Throwing herself down onto the daybed she tried to calm her racing thoughts and, after a while, dozed off to the calming sound of the ocean.

Hunger woke her and she was gratified to find a little tray, laid out and placed on the side table, containing breads and antipasti. She indulged her fill and took the tray through to the kitchen, hoping to find Nobu so that she could press her for information about Anthony, but she was nowhere to be seen.

Well, Racquel gave herself a mental shake, she was on vacation in the most stunning spot, she should relax and enjoy her own company, that had, after all, been her original plan.

There followed a peaceful afternoon of browsing magazines and sunning gently but, as the sun began to lower in the sky, Racquel found her thoughts drifting back, time and again, to Anthony.

Her body felt on high alert, sexually, the whole time. The ache in her nipples seemed to be a permanent fixture and she had to resist touching herself between her legs to alleviate the longing that throbbed there. She couldn't remember when she had last felt like this, so sexually charged, so desperate to be totally ravaged by a man.

Honey McGregor

The Shower Scene

Deciding to take a shower she walked through to her bedroom, dropping her bikini top and shorts on the floor, before stepping under the cascading water. Even the water seemed to be torturing her sexually as its needles hit her nipples and they hardened instantly. She stood there soaping her body and imagining Anthony being in the shower with her, touching her, probing her. Lifting the handheld shower head she rinsed the soap from between her legs, leaning back against the tiled wall , her hand washing the soap from her breasts under the overhead shower as she parted her legs to allow the pressure of the water to caress her below.

She could feel him touching her naked body, his hands sliding down her smooth skin, his lips kissing her neck and breasts as his fingers touched and stroked her pussy. Moaning she came suddenly, her pelvis arching forward to push against the shower head, her own wetness mixing with the wetness of the water.

Weakly she closed the faucets and stepped from the shower, wrapping a huge, fluffy, towel around herself and walking to the window to gaze out. What had happened to her? She had turned into a sex starved creature over the last couple of days. She could never remember feeling so constantly aroused.

Anthony smiled to himself. She was perfect! What a pleasure Racquel was turning out to be. He could never be absolutely sure how things would go when he made his selection but he had definitely got it right this time. His eyes lingered on the screen, watching Racquel as she stood at the window. He was pleased that he'd installed the new shower camera, just in time for Racquel to perform so beautifully for him. He wondered how long it would take for her to find the gift he'd arranged to be left in her room for her, and what her reaction would be.

Sighing, Racquel turned and, opening the closet, perused the various items of clothing hanging there. What to wear? She would be alone so there was no need to dress up. On a whim she selected the sheer kaftan, slipping it over her head to fall just below her bottom. She was beginning to enjoy this feeling of freedom with her body, not needing to wear underwear, to feel womanly and sexy, even if she was alone. She paused to look in the full-length mirror, liking what she saw, the sheer fabric making no secret of her dark nipples and dark pubic hairs. If only Anthony was here to see me, she thought wistfully.

Padding back through to the lounge she poured herself a drink and took a seat out on the patio to watch the sunset. Crossing her legs, she noticed that the kaftan had slipped up to expose her silky pubic hairs, the only covering for her aching and hungry sex. Immediately she knew that she was wet again and had to fight the desire to touch herself, so instant was her feeling of arousal.

After her second drink she sought out the welcome folder in her room, intending to read everything for any clues regarding Anthony and the workings of the island. She found it on the small bedside table and, as she picked it up, noticed a length of red silk hanging out of the drawer. Frowning slightly, she opened the drawer and smiled, another gift! Taking it out to the patio she sat down and prepared to open it, filled with anticipation. There was a small card fixed to the wrapping.

I'm sorry we couldn't finish what we started earlier... A

Fingers trembling slightly, she unwrapped the small package and took out a box. *The Silver Swan.* She blushed as she realised what it was. She'd heard of Rabbit Vibrators, of course, but she'd never used one! She placed the box down on the table and poured herself another drink, *her third*, as her mind raced. She felt so embarrassed, so naïve, like a school girl... Did Anthony expect her to use it? *Well obviously...* but on her own? With him?

The box seemed to stare at her, from its position on the little table beside her, and, feeling a little silly, she picked it up and took it back into the bedroom, placing it in the drawer again.

Finishing her drink, out on the patio, Racquel shivered slightly and realised that a breeze had got up and that she was feeling rather hungry. No doubt Nobu had everything under control though. She wandered inside, closing the door behind her, and realised that the small dining table had been set for her, a basket of fresh bread and a bottle of wine chilling in an ice bucket, completing the setting. With no sign of Nobu she walked through to the little kitchen and found a card on the counter, directing her to the refrigerator. Inside she found a delicious looking salad platter topped with pieces of avocado, bacon, haloumi and feta. She carried it to the table and served herself a generous portion, it was surprising how her appetite had picked up on Dina!

Feeling full from her meal, and deciding to forego Nobu's delightful looking raspberry mousse sitting temptingly in the fridge, at least for now, she carried the bottle of wine to the coffee table and sat down on the couch with her glass. Picking up a magazine she leafed through it, but found her thoughts drifting. She couldn't stop thinking about the vibrator nestling in the drawer beside the bed. Suddenly she made a decision and stood up, walking thought to the bedroom and opening the drawer.

Anthony was towelling himself dry after his shower when he wandered back to the bank of monitors and checked to see where Racquel was. Aha, she was fetching the vibrator, he had a feeling she would be intrigued by it, and would, hopefully, find it irresistible. His eyes followed her progress as she slowly walked back through to the lounge with the vibrator and sat back on the couch.

His phone buzzed and he picked it up distractedly, wanting to stay and watch Racquel, but it was his twin brother Charles, and they never ignored each other.

'Hi,' he answered curtly, hoping Charles didn't want a long chat. 'That's no way to answer the phone to your brother,' Charles sounded in high spirits. 'What's the problem? Is our current guest distracting you too much? I'm not surprised, I must say, she's a real beauty, and perfect in every way. So responsive...'

Anthony felt a rush of irritation and sighed, he wished Charles would respect his privacy, and that of Racquel's, but it had never bothered him before. 'Do you have to constantly spy on my guest Charles?' he asked irritably, 'I've haven't watched yours for more than about two minutes, since she arrived.'

'That's your call little brother,' (*little*, it grated when he called him that, little by about two minutes, it hardly counted...) 'But are you sure you're not a little too taken with this one? Remember the rules, *our rules*?'

It was true, Anthony thought, he *was* taken with Racquel. Suddenly the voyeuristic game he and his brother played out together didn't seem so appealing. But there was no way he was going to admit that to Charles, he must play it casually. 'No, of course not,' he replied calmly, 'I'm just enjoying myself, that's all.'

'Well that's good then,' stated Charles, before announcing 'because I'm coming over tomorrow to sample our lovely little Racquel myself, and you'd better get yourself over here to attend to our rather tasty Tanya. You'd better have a look at her tonight and familiarise yourself with her. We don't want you to blow our cover because you've been too preoccupied with your Racquel, little brother.'

Anthony's heart sank, why did he let Charles bully him so? It had always been the same, ever since their father had died, Charles had taken the lead, made all the decisions, with Anthony following along.

'Yes, Charles,' I'll check on Tanya, 'but she's not really my type, you chose her, not me. My choice this time was Racquel, can't we just keep to our choices for once? Charles' laugh sounded harshly in his ear, 'Oh no, we swap tomorrow, I'll be over at 11am, make sure you are too. And I can't wait for dinner tomorrow evening, which I understand is confirmed... and by the looks of Racquel right now, she can't wait either!'

Charles rang off, his laughter still ringing in Anthony's ear as he turned back to the monitor and Racquel.

Unbeknown to Racquel, her examination of the vibrator had been witnessed by both men on their monitors. So too had the first touch onto herself. It had felt surprisingly good. Her legs had virtually opened themselves as soon as she'd touched the vibrating object onto her clitoris and she'd felt an immediate rush of excitement deep inside.

For some strange reason she'd stopped suddenly. Not sure why, she put the vibrator down on the couch guiltily and stood up, looking around. It was crazy, she had this strange sensation of being watched, on a deserted island! Well, deserted apart from Anthony and very few staff, surely. She locked the patio doors and closed the drapes. There, no-one could see her now!

She resumed her position on the couch and allowed her legs to fall slightly apart, her sheer kaftan riding up to reveal her dark pubic hairs, and picked up the vibrator again.

Anthony held his breath as he watched Racquel slowly place the vibrator between her legs. She was so beautiful, so innocent too, so different from the kinds of women his and Charles' father had surrounded them with from such a young age. For the first time he felt slightly uncomfortable watching Racquel, and, he realised, uncomfortable with the game he and Charles played.

Still, it was hard to draw his eyes away as Racquel began to experiment with the vibrator.

His ears could pick up the slight whirring sound as she pressed the controls and touched the clitoral stimulator against herself. Slowly, she moved the pink silicone across her clitoris, opening her legs still further. She leaned back into the couch cushions, the sheer fabric of the kaftan clearly showing her dark nipples. Tantalisingly the vibrator circled her clit, wetness beginning to glisten in her hairs, where the hem of her kaftan skimmed them. She spread her legs still further, adjusting the position of the vibrator so that the larger shaft probed the source of her wetness. Plunging it inside herself she gasped and thrust forward, her pelvis lifting upwards, and began to grind against the dual pleasure source.

Anthony was still standing in front of the monitor, naked, and realised that he was holding himself, his rock-hard penis almost straining towards the monitor and Racquel. He watched her writhe with pleasure as the hand holding his cock began to slide up and down its length. He heard her gasp as she surrendered to her orgasm and realised that he'd come too, when he felt his own wetness spilling over his hand.

He turned away from the monitor, feeling suddenly awkward in witnessing Racquel's private moments of pleasure. She trusted him and he was betraying that trust every time he secretly watched her. What had happened to him? Something had changed with Racquel's arrival on the island. More to the point, what was he going to do about it? With a sinking heart he thought of his conversation with Charles and of what tomorrow held.

Anthony washed himself and, after dressing, sat back down at the monitors, this time switching over to Naru Island and Tanya, with a heavy heart.

Charles watched Racquel pleasure herself and felt a moment of envy at the gorgeous woman his brother had selected as his latest guest on Dina. Well, he was going to enjoy her himself tomorrow, and he wasn't going to stop until he'd had her completely. Unlike Anthony, who seemed to be taking things very slowly... he hadn't even slept with her yet!

Racquel opened her eyes in surprise, she'd been so carried away with pleasure. She'd had no idea that a vibrator could provide so much satisfaction! Maybe she'd purchase one when she returned home, she thought, it would certainly help on those nights when she felt filled with frustration at being alone. Home. The word depressed her slightly, at this moment she felt as if she could live on Dina forever... with Anthony... Smiling and telling herself not to get so carried away, she stood up, collecting the vibrator, and headed to her room.

Honey McGregor

Naru

Bloody Charles, thought Anthony, as he watched his twin, so brash, just like his choice in women. Tanya was a typical example of the women their father had invited into their home when the boys were young. Over tanned, over made-up and over skinny, with false boobs. Of course, at the time it had seemed like every boy's wet dream to have a house filled with sexy women, any one of which was happy to oblige them in the pleasure department. It had been one long party, drinks flowing, music playing and his father and their friends indulging in sex with one woman after another, the two boys too.

He wondered if things would have been different if their mother had not died when they were young. Maybe so, but then again, maybe her death had spared her from the worst of their father's behaviour. But he and Charles had not been spared and he wondered now if they had not been damaged by their decadent upbringing. It had never occurred to him before, he'd always just been guided by Charles, the strong one, the bossy leader. He'd accepted his upbringing as cool, exciting, lucky even, and had perpetuated it in adulthood, taken it further in fact. Too far, he thought now, as he considered what he and Charles were doing to innocent women.

He watched Tanya shriek with laughter as Charles grabbed her and leapt into the pool with her. They were both completely drunk and having a wild party. Tanya pulled herself out of the pool and began to remove her sodden dress, in what she obviously considered a sexy manner, unaware that her mascara was making streaks down her face. Charles climbed out and dropped his shorts, so that he was naked, and grabbed hold of her dress, yanking it over her head before turning her around and leaning her over the outdoor table.

Anthony switched the monitor off, he'd had enough. Maybe some of the women weren't so innocent, he considered. Tanya was obviously having the time of her life and would, presumably, have no regrets about her exclusive and somewhat decadent vacation. Much like most of the women he'd chosen until now, he considered. He'd generally been guided by Charles and what they'd grown used to, and had selected similar women, until Racquel...

The next day dawned bright and sunny (as usual) and Racquel stretched happily in her comfortable bed. She felt filled with optimism about the day ahead, and especially the evening, her inner voice made her admit to herself. Pulling on her robe she wandered through to the kitchen where she could hear Nobu working quietly, the smell of coffee filling the air. She took the proffered mug from Nobu, smiling her thanks, and in response to Nobu's enquiry, requested eggs and bacon. She felt famished, island life definitely agreed with her!

A leisurely day followed, sunning, swimming and reading magazines, with a break for a light lunch of baguette and cheese. She felt a growing excitement at the evening ahead, she was going to give herself to Anthony completely! She would have already, she knew, if circumstances had not stopped them the last time. Showered, scented and dressed carefully in one of the dreamy dresses from the closet, together with a lacy bra and panties, she eagerly awaited Anthony's arrival as evening descended. She helped herself to a drink from the trolley on the patio and tried to relax.

Charles was also filled with a growing excitement, having arrived on Dina earlier that day and spending an enjoyable afternoon tracking Racquel's activities on the monitors, accompanied by more than a few beers. He selected some clothing from Anthony's closet, their tastes a little different, he personally preferred somewhat smarter clothes than Anthony's casual attire. He opened a bottle of wine, taking a large swig from the bottle and pouring himself a full glass to drink before he set off for his evening with Racquel.

Anthony looked around in disgust at his brother's bedroom and bathroom. He really was a pig. Even with staff to clean for him he managed to leave a trail of destruction in his wake. The differences between them were beginning to become more marked, he realised. He showered and looked for something to wear, wishing he could just keep on his frayed denims and casual shirt. But tonight he had to be Charles, those were the rules they'd agreed on, and so he selected a pair of tailored shorts, a golf shirt and a pair of leather moccasins. He sprayed on some cologne and headed off in the golf cart towards the villa where Tanya awaited Charles.

When she heard the golf cart arrive outside her villa she jumped up in anticipation and rushed to the door, eager to see Anthony. The door flew open. 'How's my beautiful Racquel this evening?' His kiss was sudden, and, as her body was pressed back against the wall under his, Racquel was taken off guard, his probing tongue inside her mouth before she'd had time to speak.

His hands roved over her body and she felt herself responding to his touch, but, at the same time, feeling slightly surprised at his sudden overt embrace. She tried to pull away, in vain, feeling unsure for the first time since she'd arrived on Dina. 'Anthony', she exclaimed, trying to laugh, as she managed to push him away, 'It's nice to see you too!' She led him through to the patio and was about to offer him a drink when she realised that he was already helping himself. Her glass was empty, she noticed, but he didn't offer to refill it for her. What had happened to him? Looking more closely at him she realised that his eyes were rather red and she realised that he had been drinking before he arrived. He was usually such a gentleman, what could have happened today to make him behave so out of character?

Anthony arrived at Tanya's villa with a sinking heart. How was he going to get through the evening? Could he even pull it off? And more worryingly, what was happening over on Dina with Racquel and Charles? How could he have left her with his brother? Suddenly it was unbearable, he couldn't stand it if Charles slept with her. It had never mattered before, the women were all the same, they were his, they were Charles', they meant nothing, just like the women they knew growing up. He turned decisively, he would take his boat back now and put a stop to this, even if it meant losing Racquel forever. But the door opened and there was Tanya, already inebriated if her glazed eyes were anything to go by, grabbing him by the collar and pulling him inside. He made a decision, he would act out the farce, for the last time, he would ply Tanya with drinks until she passed out (it shouldn't be too difficult) and then return to Dina before Charles could do any damage.

'Charles! Welcome darling, come and get a drink!' With a wet, slobbery kiss, which missed his mouth, she staggered ahead of him through the villa, her glass spilling drops onto the rug. The music was loud and she'd clearly been partying the whole afternoon, if not the whole day. He poured himself a drink and topped up her glass, smiling as he helped her into a chair.

He looked at her with distaste, her make-up was smudged, her hair messy and her dress strap was falling from one shoulder. He thought of Racquel, no doubt looking beautiful and stylish, and no doubt suffering at the hands of Charles right now. Surreptitiously checking his watch, he offered her another drink as soon as she'd drained her glass, taking care to only sip his own. It was easier than he'd thought. Tanya had staggered up, wanting to dance, and he'd kept her plied with alcohol, as she'd become more and more drunk. He wondered what his face looked like, his fixed grin probably looking pretty ghoulish, as he determined to get this woman into her bed and passed out for the night as quickly as possible.

Meanwhile, back on Dina, things were progressing strangely, at least for Racquel. Anthony didn't seem at all interested in Nobu's delightful cuisine, the beautifully laid table and food holding little interest for him. Some instinct told Racquel to slow things down, to make sure they dined, and to also make sure that she didn't drink too much this evening. She felt disappointment swamp her. It had clearly been too good to be true. The whole thing had just been a figment of her imagination, inspired by her beautiful surroundings. How else could someone change so much overnight?

Anthony's plan was going well, but he hadn't factored one event in, couldn't possibly have. This was when Tanya tripped and managed to gash her head on the side of the pool as she'd tried to drunkenly pull him in with her for a skinny dip. The effort of removing her dress, kicking off her shoes, and trying to pull

Anthony with her had caused the unfortunate accident and he was now beholden to make sure that she was alright. He bathed her wound, which fortunately wasn't deep after all, and helped her to bed, having made sure that she wasn't acting strangely and didn't need to go to hospital on the mainland. He waited with her for an hour after she fell asleep, impatiently checking his watch the whole time, until he felt he could justify leaving her and returning to Dina.

Charles was bored. Racquel might look inviting but this whole dinner thing was dragging. She'd hardly touched her wine and he was acutely aware of the fact that he was now pretty drunk. He forced some food down and was relieved when she agreed to leave the table and relax on the patio with after dinner drinks. It was now or never. He lunged at Racquel, pulling at the straps of her dress and kissing her firmly on the mouth.

Anthony rushed up to his villa and went straight to his monitors, anxious to see what was happening with Racquel and his twin. His jaw twitched with irritation when he saw Charles lunge at her out on the patio. Angrily he grabbed his keys to head straight there, regardless of the consequences, when he heard Racquel shout out. Pausing to check, he watched Racquel push Charles off of her and jump up, begging him to leave. But Charles was not to be thwarted and he grabbed Racquel, throwing her onto the day bed and lowering himself on top of her.

Racquel couldn't believe this was happening, how could Anthony be so different suddenly? Why wasn't he respecting her wishes? She struggled underneath him, tears running down her face as she tried to stop him pulling her dress straps down. Her dress had ridden up and his one hand was now tugging at her panties, as she desperately struggled to stop him. 'Please, Anthony,' she begged, 'don't do this, not like this.'

Suddenly Anthony seemed to rise up in the air and fall backwards, a look of surprise on his face. His surprise was nothing compared to the surprise on Racquel's face as she looked at Anthony being pulled away by... *Anthony?* She gasped in shock and huddled back into the day bed cushions as the two Anthony's struggled.

'I'm through with this, Charles, it's over,' shouted Anthony, as he pulled his brother away, twisting his arms behind his back. 'I'm not playing your games any more, I'm done!'

Charles squirmed against Anthony's hold on him, but anger must have given Anthony extra strength, as Charles felt helpless, no doubt helped by the number of drinks he'd had already. 'It's not over Anthony, you need me! You've always needed me!'

'Not anymore!' Anthony pulled him away from Racquel and began to drag him towards the door, looking apologetically at Racquel and telling her he'd be back soon to explain.

Explain what? Racquel's mind was whirring in total confusion. Two Anthonys. But one of them was called Charles? Twins, it must be, of course! There was no other explanation, but how had Anthony's twin taken his place for the evening? And where had her Anthony been? With shaking hands, she fixed herself a drink and sank back down onto the day bed as she heard more arguing and the golf cart heading off.

Anthony glanced grimly over at Charles who was nursing his jaw where Anthony had finally punched him, just once but enough to subdue him. He drove to the little harbour where both boats sat bobbing on the water and switched off the engine. 'Get out,' he glared at Charles, 'go back to Naru, we'll talk tomorrow. But I meant what I said, I'm through with all this.'

Charles staggered out of the golf cart and headed to his boat. 'You'll change your mind little brother, you need me, you'll see.'

Anthony waited just long enough to make sure that Charles was leaving and then resolutely set off back to Racquel. How was he going to explain? She'd never forgive him, that was for sure. But something had snapped inside him and he knew that he had to try to make things right.

Honey McGregor

Dead Ringers

Racquel look up as she heard footsteps coming through the villa to the patio. 'Anthony?'

'Yes, it's really me,' Anthony looked at her anxiously, 'I'm so sorry Racquel, I don't know where to begin, but first I have to attend to some practical matters.' He was holding a bunch of keys and she followed him as he unlocked a cupboard that she'd barely noticed, just inside the entrance of the villa. He fiddled with various switches and then, satisfied, closed the cupboard. 'Do you mind if I fix myself a drink? You look like you could do with one too.'

Yes, that's Anthony, thought Racquel, he at least has manners. She let him lead her back through to the patio, where he fixed them drinks, and then to lower her to one of the chairs as he took a seat beside her.

Anthony gently took her hand. 'Racquel, I cannot apologise enough for my twin brother's behaviour. But I have to apologise for so much more than that and I don't quite know where to start.'

He looked so troubled that her heart softened. Whatever it was, he deserved the right to explain it to her. 'Why don't you start at the beginning,' she said softly, smiling into his eyes, hoping desperately that it was something she could at least make sense of.

Taking a deep breath, and a large gulp of whisky, Anthony began.

'When my twin bother, Charles, and I were young, our mother died. Our father was very wealthy, proceeds from his lucrative film production career, and we didn't want for anything. At least that's what I always thought. We were the envy of all our friends, we lived in a big mansion with little or no supervision. Our father enjoyed a decadent lifestyle and brought home constant streams of friends, life was one big party.'

He looked at Racquel anxiously. 'The friends were both men and women. The women were,' he paused, 'I never questioned it, they were, at least I always thought they were, actresses, maybe they'd acted in his movies, or wanted to. They just wanted to party, the drinks flowed, drugs too, and we were just encouraged to be a part of it. We felt so cool, so grown-up, sometimes we'd invite our friends round as well, and that just elevated our status in their eyes. My father imposed no rules on us, even encouraged us, and Charles and I did whatever we wanted to. Do you understand what I'm trying to say Racquel?' His pained expression tugged at her heart as she murmured that she did.

'Go on,' she whispered quietly.

'It was total decadence, at times one big orgy, the women were there for our entertainment, they never said no, to us it was normal. Very often Charles would take a woman and then pass her on to me, saying that what was his was mine and vice versa. I never questioned it, I was young.'

Racquel's heart contracted, he looked so pained. 'You were young Anthony, the way your father brought you up was wrong, it damaged you, but it's not your fault.' But where was this going? she wondered anxiously.

Anthony took another gulp of his whisky. 'Racquel, it is my fault, I should never have listened to Charles, should never have let him lead me.' 'But you can't blame yourself for what happened tonight!' she exclaimed, her gentle face looking at him so caringly.

Taking a deep breath Anthony continued. 'My father died when we were still young, in our twenties, and Charles and I inherited his fortune. And I really mean a fortune. For a while we just continued in the same lifestyle, the same faces still came to our home, the parties continued, life just went on. And then Charles had this idea. He wanted us to sell the house and buy two small islands, one for him and one for me. He organised everything, the purchasing of the islands, the building of the villas, everything.' He looked at her pleadingly.

Two islands? She looked at him enquiringly. 'What d'you mean two islands Anthony?'

'Dina and Naru', he said. I live on Dina and Charles lives on Naru. It only takes us about five minutes by boat to visit each other's island. Each island has two villas, one for us to live in and one for our guests.'

Racquel stood up. 'So, does this mean that Charles also has a guest? A woman like me, on a vacation? And why would he come to your island and pretend to be you?' Her voice was rising as she began to imagine the worst. 'Do you share us?' Her look of horror pierced at Anthony's heart. 'Were you on his island last night with his guest? How could you, it's just sick!' She paced up and down the patio as she imagined what she had unwittingly become a part of. 'Oh my God! It's just like that movie, Dead Ringers, with sick twins both using the same women! You're sick! You're both sick! And perverted!' With that she turned and fled, heading for her bedroom where he heard the door slam.

The full realisation of just how wrong what he and Charles had been doing washed over Anthony as he sat there nursing his drink. Unsure of what to do he tentatively walked to the bedroom door and knocked gently. 'Racquel, please let me come in.' He could hear her sobbing and wanted, more than anything, to ease her pain. But how could he, when he was the very cause of it.

Her door opened and he looked into her tear-stained face. 'Please,' he begged, 'let me finish, I need to tell you everything.' Slowly, Racquel walked out of the room and into the lounge, seating herself on the couch. She nodded silently and so he continued with his confession.

34

'It's true that I was on Charles's island last night, but I swear to you that nothing happened with his guest. I didn't want to go, even begged Charles to leave you alone. Something changed when you arrived on Dina. *I* changed. But Charles insisted, and he's always been the leader, there's not been a day in my life that I've not done what he's said. I know that sounds weak, but we're twins, we've always been so close and I never questioned Charles' decisions before last night. But he'd seen you and he was determined to be with you, nothing was going to stop him.'

'Wait!' Racquel's eyes glinted dangerously. 'What d'you mean he'd seen me? How could he have? And what were you doing in that cupboard, with all those switches, when you said you had to do something earlier?' Her mind was beginning to think the absolute worst. Surely not though. It couldn't be that they'd been... *watching* her?' She jumped up suddenly, her hand cupped over her mouth, and rushed to the bathroom.

Anthony followed, the sounds of her gagging filling him with a terrible remorse. How could he have done this to such a beautiful and gentle woman? She didn't deserve it. He poured her some water from the jug in the bedroom and handed it to her silently, waiting for her to compose herself as best she could.

Racquel's eyes were travelling wildly over the ceiling and around the room. 'Where are they?' her voice rasped, 'Where are the cameras? Show me.'

Silently Anthony pointed out where the hidden cameras were, one by one, until he'd covered the whole villa and patio. 'They're all switched off now, no-one can see you, you have my word.' My word, he thought bitterly, what good is my word after what I've done to Racquel?

'I want you to go now,' Racquel felt swamped with exhaustion and just wanted to be left alone. She wanted to curl up in bed and forget about the sick game she'd become a part of. 'Please go,' she whispered.

Helplessly, Anthony turned to go. 'Can I come to you tomorrow? To talk?' Silently she nodded, before entering her bedroom and closing the door. He left, heading back to his villa with a feeling of total desolation. He'd see Racquel tomorrow but he knew that it would make no difference. He would lose her. She'd been the catalyst that had made him see just how wrong his life with Charles was, she was also the woman that he wanted to share his life with, he realised. And, he realised, with chilling finality, he was never going to get to do that.

Racquel lay in her bed, her eyes sore from crying, and thought back over her short time at Villa Tali. It had seemed so perfect, she'd felt so happy, and now she knew that it was all a sick game played out by the two brothers. The vacation website! That was how they lured their prey, she realised. All those questions designed to tailor make your vacation, your likes and dislikes, your photo submitted, *so they could have a good look at you...* And the joy when you were accepted!

How many women, she wondered bitterly, had been disappointed when their application was rejected, unknowingly saved from this perverse, sexual, game.

Finally, Racquel fell asleep and was surprised to find her room filled with sunlight, and it to already be mid-morning, when she next opened her eyes. She threw the bed covers back and stepped out of bed, then hesitated, conscious that she was naked. She glanced frantically up at where she now knew the hidden cameras were, and grabbed her gown, not trusting Anthony's promise that they were all switched off. The smell of coffee lured her to the kitchen where she found a fresh jug waiting for her, as well as warm croissants and jam. Wondering whether Nobu was aware of just how wrong the whole arrangement was, she helped herself and breakfasted quickly out on the patio.

Her shower was a hurried affair, anxiety about cameras making her uncomfortable, and she quickly dressed, wondering how soon she could leave the island.

Anthony spent a tortured night at his villa before taking his boat over to Naru Island early in the morning. He need to confront Charles and make him realise that he'd meant what he'd said the night before. He really was through with it all. Any appeal the excitement had held for him had gone, he wanted to begin life again with a clean slate. He'd lost Racquel, that much was obvious, but he felt free of Charles' control for the first time in his life.

Charles was nursing a hangover and drinking strong coffee when Anthony arrived. 'Hey little brother, you really blew it last night. You could've ruined everything, all our fun, our whole lifestyle. What were you thinking?'

Anthony poured himself some coffee and sat down opposite Charles. 'I hope I have ruined it all Charles, I want no part of this anymore. I can't believe I went along with everything you suggested for so long. We're through. I've already closed down our website, that's it, no more vacations for lonely women. It's time we went our separate ways, I need to grow up, something I should have done years ago. And I need to do it on my own, without you.

Charles sighed, 'Well, I suppose I knew there would always come a time when my little brother wouldn't need me anymore. We've had some fun though, we've been a good team! But what are you going to do? Run off into the sunset with your Racquel?'

'I wish,' said Anthony sadly. 'No, there's no hope of that, but I am going to try to ask her forgiveness today, before she leaves, for leave she will, I've no doubt.'

Racquel's bags were packed when Anthony arrived at her villa and she opened the door to him without a smile. 'When can I leave?' she asked abruptly.

'I'll organise the pilot as soon as I return to my villa,' he assured her. 'I just wanted to make sure that you were alright, and to ask you to forgive me, even though I have no right to.'

He looked so dejected that her heart melted, just a little. Careful, Racquel, she admonished herself, this pervert has been spying on you. Nonetheless, with flawless manners she offered him some coffee, pouring them both a cup when he accepted.

She watched him covertly, as he drank his coffee. He was so handsome, so perfect, she'd wanted him so badly… He was the first man she'd allowed to get close to her in so many years, she'd truly felt that he was beginning to care for her. She knew that she'd certainly been beginning to care for him. Suddenly she wanted to see his villa, to see where he'd spied on her from, to try to understand the whole set-up, before she left, never to see him again.

Anthony was surprised at her request, but felt no right to refuse her. He owed her full transparency now, it was the least he could do.

He led her into his villa, noting her enquiring glances around, and the look of approval that flicked over her face, before it turned to distaste at the sight of the computer monitors on the large desk. They were all switched off, of course, he'd even dismantled the master switch so that Charles couldn't possibly access anything.

'This is where you watched me?' she whispered, looking up at him with her sad eyes.

He nodded, feeling terrible. 'Yes, I'm afraid it is.'

'How many? How many women have you watched? How many women have you seduced?'

'Please, Racquel, please don't let me make it worse for you. Isn't it enough that I did this to you? I feel so ashamed, I'd give anything to make it that this never happened.'

'It's too late,' she sighed, 'I need to go now Anthony.'

Honey McGregor

The Departure

Georges, the chauffeur, delivered her to the light aircraft and waiting pilot and Racquel boarded the small plane, wondering at how different she felt now to the day she'd arrived. It had only been, what, three days? How would she explain it to Stella? She could never tell her the truth!

In the event, she hadn't needed to explain anything to Stella. Apparently Stella had tried to suggest the same vacation to another friend 'in need', but had read the latest review, by 'Tanya', describing the whole experience as *one long drunken party, just what she'd needed, crazy fun, great sex and a totally wild time!*

'I'm so sorry, my darling,' she'd apologised, 'I really had no idea it could be like that. I never intended anything like that for you. I thought it was an exclusive, tasteful, vacation. I decided to contact the company to complain, but it appears that they've closed down. The website's gone, everything. There's no way of contacting them at all. Where was the island even? It never actually said.'

With a sinking heart, Racquel listened to Stella, and her heart sank even further when she realised that she didn't actually know where the island was. Everything had been taken care of, that was the whole point. She'd had no need to think of, or organise, anything.

Months passed and Racquel couldn't shake her depression. With a jolt she realised that she missed Anthony. She tried to push the thought away, how could she miss a man who'd lied to her, spied on her and taken his sexual gratification with her, all the time knowing that his brother was watching her too?

The more she tried to stop thinking of him, the more her mind played tricks on her. The nights became torture, she'd toss and turn, memories of his touch, and how he made her feel, driving her crazy. One night she awoke from a dream of him to find herself in the throes of an orgasm, wetness between her legs and a throbbing desire that wouldn't go away.

Tentatively she touched herself, slipping her finger inside to coat it in her wetness, before gently stroking it over her sensitive clitoris. She was naked, a habit she'd continued since leaving Dina, and she threw back the covers as her pelvis pushed upwards, images of Anthony flooding her mind, and her finger moving faster as she reached her climax and came with a sigh.

She'd begun to drive herself crazy with her internet searches, examining every website offering exclusive vacations on an island, in the mad hope that maybe the brothers were still up to their tricks. And then? What would that achieve? More torture at the thought of Anthony with other women, seducing them, like he seduced her... And when she found nothing, she felt equally despondent, because she knew it meant that she would never see him again...

Anthony drove slowly past the driveway to Racquel's house, catching a glimpse of the building at the end of it. It had been six months. Six months in which he'd not spoken to Charles. Six months in which he'd thought of Racquel every single day. Finally, his obsession had got the better of him and he'd travelled to her home town. For the past week he'd been staying in a hotel nearby, driving past her house every day, hoping to catch sight of her. He pulled in further down the road and his head dropped to his chest. What was he doing? She'd never want to see him. And if she knew he'd been driving past her house she'd just see it as stalking, which it was really. It was as bad as when he'd spied on her on Dina.

A movement in his mirror caught his eye and he saw a red car leaving her driveway. His heart beat rapidly, it must be Racquel! Turning his face away as she drove past, he slowly followed her, unable to resist the chance of actually seeing her, even if only from a distance.

He pulled into the mall parking and parked his car a row behind hers, waiting for her to leave her car before he followed, keeping his distance in case she turned around. But Racquel walked slowly, looking straight ahead, with no suspicions.

Feeling embarrassed, Racquel entered the store, its window filled with displays of lingerie clad mannequins. She drifted between the racks of underwear, picking up various items, putting them back, and then pausing at a selection of wispy thongs. They reminded her of the thong she'd worn with the pale gold dress, the night she'd been seduced by Anthony, her first night on Dina.

She picked one up, and, keeping hold of it, moved on to the displays towards the back of the store. This wasn't her first visit, she'd been in twice before, but this time she was going to leave with what she'd come for. There they were, vibrators and other items, all discreetly packaged. She watched as another woman casually browsed the selection, examining various vibrators before choosing one and heading for the counter to pay. She showed no embarrassment, and the girl on the counter showed no interest in what her customer was buying, ringing up the purchase and taking payment with barely a glance at the package, as she placed it inside a bag.

Taking a deep breath Racquel picked up the Silver Swan and took it to the counter, together with the wispy thong, and walked out of the store a moment later.

Dina Island

Anthony watched in surprise as Racquel entered the store, and then felt a flash of jealousy, she must be buying something to wear for a man. Unable to help himself he walked inside and browsed the items of sheer and lacy clothing, murmuring something about his wife's birthday when an assistant asked if he needed any help. He watched Racquel pick up the thong with a sinking heart, yes, it must be for a man. Glued to the spot, his eyes followed her to the displays of vibrators, his heart lightening when he saw her select the Silver Swan. Maybe not a man after all... Quickly, he turned around and left the store, so that she didn't see him, taking up a position behind a large, leafy plant, in the centre of the walkway.

Her beautiful face tore at his heart as she walked by, she was as gorgeous as he remembered, even more so. She looked sad, but determined, as she headed back to her car.

Suddenly feeling excited, Anthony continued on in the mall, making a purchase in the perfume store before heading to the florist.

Strange, thought Racquel, she wasn't expecting anyone. She answered the door enquiringly and smiled in surprise at the delivery man holding the enormous arrangement of red roses. 'Someone's birthday?' he smiled, asking her to sign for the flowers.

Flustered, she shook her head, smiling her thanks as she closed the door and carried the enormous arrangement to the lounge. There was a small package tucked in among the roses and she lifted it out, unwrapping it and gasping at its contents. Chanel Cristalle! She'd worn it on Dina. With Anthony! She sprayed some on her wrists, inhaling its fresh fragrance, memories swirling around in her head. What did this mean? Frantically she rummaged through the roses, looking for a card, but found nothing. They must be from him! And red roses! There'd been a beautiful arrangement of red roses in her lounge at Villa Tali... Excitement bubbled up inside her.

Back at his hotel Anthony nursed his whisky at the bar. He looked at his watch, she must have the roses by now, and the perfume. Would she know they were from him? But more to the point, how would she feel? Would she discard them in disgust? Or would they make her happy?

Racquel found herself humming as she took her shower, lazily soaping herself under the hot jets of water. A memory of her shower on Dina came to her, when she had pleasured herself with thoughts of Anthony. She traced her fingers lightly across her nipples and down lower, into her small, silken bush, gently touching herself between her legs. It felt good, *she* felt good she realised, and she knew why. It was because of him. She knew he was close. She knew he must be watching her...

With surprise she realised that the thought of Anthony watching her was arousing. Of course, she knew he couldn't actually be watching her *now*...

41

feeling silly she looked up at the ceiling, no, of course not, this was her home, not his villa, there were no hidden cameras here. Still...

Once she was dry she spritzed on the Chanel Cristalle liberally, wanting to keep the feeling of Anthony close. *I miss him*, she admitted to herself. *I miss him and I care about him. I even find the idea of him watching me a turn on. I wish he was watching me now as I slip on this wispy thong that reminds me so much of him.*

Her eyes fell on the package that she'd placed on the bed earlier. Feeling suddenly free and light-hearted she picked it up and went downstairs, pouring herself a glass of wine.

Anthony could wait no longer. He picked up his phone and typed in a message, deliberating for a moment before pressing send. And then he waited, heart pounding, as he ordered another whisky.

The evening was unusually sultry, and in her new, liberated state of mind, Racquel slid open the patio doors and walked outside with her wine. The feel of the warm air on her near naked body felt good and she reclined on her cushioned couch, placing the package down beside her.

Her phone buzzed and she picked it up, reading the message from *unknown* with a racing heart.

Did you like the roses?

It was from him! It had to be! With trembling fingers she replied.

I love them!

Are you wearing the Cristalle?

I am x

She'd put a kiss at the end, that must mean something...

I miss you... x

He missed her, and he'd put a kiss at the end too, that must mean something...

I miss you too... she stopped. She wanted to see him so badly. Nothing else mattered any more. She no longer cared about what had happened, they could fix it, she was sure.

Where are you? x

I'm five minutes away... tell me you want me and I'll come... x

I want you... but I want you my way... x

Anything you want...x

There's a small lane at the end of my garden. Wait at the little gate. I want you to watch me... x

Watching

He stood at the little gate, looking up at her patio lit by the outside light. He could barely breathe. She looked so beautiful. She was virtually naked, wearing only the lacy thong he'd seen her purchase earlier. She was holding the pink vibrator, a small smile playing on her lips as she glanced towards the little gate.

He was there, she could sense him! She'd never felt so hot in her life! She wanted him to watch her as she touched her body, as she played with herself... as she came... and then she wanted him inside her...

Her hand slowly stroked her naked body, gently touching her nipples and then moving lower, her legs opening to accommodate her fingers as they reached for her central core of desire. She touched herself through the fine fabric of the thong, silky wetness instantly soaking through to her fingers. She groaned, it all felt so good... and to know that Anthony was watching her... all her inhibitions had gone... she wanted to do this for him, for her... for them... to show him that it was alright, that she understood, she'd forgiven him...

With her other hand she placed the vibrator between her legs and moved slowly against the soft vibrating head, parting her legs further as she became even more turned on.

Anthony watched, heavy with desire, as Racquel writhed and moaned, the silicone sliding over her wetness, her pelvis pushing forwards with her own desire. Her free hand moved to touch her small, firm, breasts, her nipples jutting out with her arousal. She moved the vibrator and lifted herself up slightly to pull her panties to one side, as she pushed the larger part inside her, moving rhythmically now as she approached her orgasm.

He was rock hard, could feel his own wetness beginning to seep through his jeans, as he watched, mesmerised. He could hear her gasps as she began to come, and could wait no longer. Opening the gate, he walked quickly up the path to her.

Racquel could sense him in front of her and opened her eyes. She was still coming when he gently took the vibrator from her hand and removed it, replacing her yearning with his hand. He lifted her up and pulled her close to him, his lips pressing onto hers as her mouth opened, and he slid his tongue inside, tasting her again, after so long.

Her body juddered against his as his hand cupped her and received the last creamy remnants of her orgasm.

Silently they looked into each other's eyes as Anthony picked her up, dropping the vibrator onto the cushions.

'That's the last time you'll ever need that,' he smiled lovingly into her eyes as he carried her into the house and up the stairs to the bedroom.

Racquel lay in a daze as Anthony pulled his clothes off, his beautiful naked body standing proudly in front of her. Her eyes fell to his cock, huge and hard in front of her, ready for her, and she opened her arms invitingly, smiling happily as he began to kiss her again.

Finally, they made love, kissing and touching each other all over, gasping with pleasure as they explored each other's bodies. Anthony's lips moved slowly over Racquel's body, kissing and teasing as he went, until, slipping her thong down her legs and onto the floor, his tongue probed her soaking pussy. She pushed herself onto his tongue, wanting it to slide inside, but he moved back up her body, his fingers gently probing her instead, as he kissed and sucked her nipples.

They rolled over and Racquel, now on top, began to kiss Anthony's firm chest, enjoying the sound of his groans as she moved lower, to take him in her mouth and slide her tongue over his cock, teasing and sucking his taste and wetness.

Anthony's hands were buried in Racquel's hair and, as she moved back up to kiss him, he held her hair from her face as they gazed at each other. 'Are you ready?' he asked, and, when she nodded, he rolled her over, so that she was underneath him again, before finally plunging inside her. They moved together perfectly, carried away with their desire for each other, holding, kissing, gasping and finally coming together with a joint cry.

Return to Dina

Racquel stepped from the light aircraft, remembering the last time she'd been here. She turned and smiled at Anthony as he took her hand.

'Welcome back Mr Baron. Welcome back Mrs Hampton.' Georges smiled as he opened the doors of the jeep for them.

'Actually it's Mrs Baron now,' grinned Anthony, as Georges exclaimed in excitement and congratulated them both.

As they walked into Anthony's villa, Racquel's gaze fell on his monitors, remembering how distraught she'd felt the last time she was here. Anthony's arms reached around her from behind, 'Are you okay?' he asked worriedly. She smiled, looking up at him, 'I'm fine my darling, 'I was just wondering if these still worked, you know, the cameras at Villa Tali and everything?'

Anthony turned her around in his arms, so that they were facing each other, 'They do, but they're all switched off at the villa, ever since that day... why do you ask?' 'Oh nothing,' she smiled mysteriously, 'just an idea I had...'

'Is Nobu organised for our meal this evening?' asked Racquel a little later, as she dried her hair after her shower.

'Oh yes, everything will be prepared for us, as per your request, but we could have dined here you know.' Anthony reached for her naked body, pulling her towards him and kissing her, his hands running over her hips as his erection took hold.

But Racquel wriggled from his grasp, laughing. 'Not yet, I have plans for you later!' She disappeared off to the bedroom to dress and Anthony marvelled at how relaxed and happy she was. He still couldn't believe how things had worked out, he thought, as he followed and selected his clothes for the evening.

Before they set off to Villa Tali, Racquel asked Anthony again about the monitors. 'Do they also record?' she wanted to know.

'Racquel, darling, why are you asking about all this after it caused so many problems? Shouldn't we forget about it and start afresh?'

But Racquel was insistent and so Anthony showed her how he could set the monitors to record, if he wished, although he assured her that he had never used the facility.

As they were about to set off in the golf cart, Racquel exclaimed, 'Oh, I forgot my purse! I won't be a moment.' She rushed back inside and returned, a minute or two later with her purse. 'Let's go!' she sighed happily, 'I'm so looking forward to our first evening together, back on Dina Island!'

Nobu's grin was enormous as she welcomed them both at Villa Tali, with a hug for Racquel at their happy news. Once she'd left, Racquel looked around, filled with happiness, she did so love this villa, and the events of her last visit were a distant memory now, not bothering her at all. She took Anthony's hand as they wandered through to the patio to take in the view and Nobu's beautifully laid table. 'Everything's perfect!' Anthony grinned happily at her enthusiasm, 'I can't quite believe this is happening,' he said, as he pulled her close.

The evening was beyond perfect, the champagne before dinner was chilled to perfection, as was the wine with dinner. Nobu had surpassed herself, her cold starter, of beef carpaccio, light and delicate, filled with flavour, her main course extracting gasps of pleasure. 'How does Nobu do it? This salmon is so tender, and the pureed garlic potato is heavenly...' They both leaned back in their chairs, feeling perfectly satisfied, but agreeing to just sample the delicious dessert, after Nobu had gone to so much trouble.

Anthony held his spoon to Racquel's lips as she licked the last of the chocolate mousse from it, watching her with increasing desire. She was so beautiful, and sexy, she made even the simple act of licking a spoon erotic... and the most amazing thing was that she seemed so unaware of her desirability, so natural...

'What are you thinking?' Racquel asked quietly, smiling at him.

'I was thinking just how sexy my wife is,' grinned Anthony, 'and that maybe we should take our cognac to the day bed...'

As Anthony purred them both a cognac, Racquel hovered, wanting to ask him   something. 'Anthony,' she began, tentatively, 'I want to switch the cameras on.' He looked at her in complete surprise, handing her a glass of cognac. 'But why? I nearly lost you forever because of those cameras, why would you ever want me to switch them on again?'

She took his free hand, 'Those cameras did nearly destroy us, it's true, but I didn't know you were watching me. And then, when I asked you to watch me in my garden I felt so turned on, the thought of you watching me was amazing. Now I want us to watch ourselves, knowingly, it's perfect!'

Anthony shook his head in amazement, his wife was full of surprises. 'But I didn't switch on the monitors to record at my villa. Wait a minute, you forgot your purse... you went back in... did you...?' Her grin told him everything and, handing her his glass to hold, he moved to the entrance hall, opening the cupboard and switching on the various switches.

They lay back on the cushions of the day bed together, sipping their cognac, both aware of the camera recording them. Racquel turned to Anthony, 'Take my glass, like you did that first time...' He took it, placing it down with his, on the side table and turned back to her, taking her in his arms.

'Are you absolutely sure you want to do this?' he looked so concerned. She nodded, 'It's my way of telling you that everything is alright. I forgive you, none of what happened before matters. This is our new start, it's my gift to you, and...,' she whispered sexily, ' I'm also finding it very arousing...'

Slowly, he began to unfasten the little pearl buttons that held her dress together, her small breasts appearing invitingly before him. He lowered his mouth to first one nipple and then the other, Racquel's gentle moans sounding in his ears. She buried her face in his hair, breathing in his scent, before kissing him slowly when he raised his face to hers, their tongues exploring each other's mouths languorously.

His hard cock pressed into her mound and she pushed herself against him, feeling herself becoming wet with desire.

Suddenly Anthony pulled back and looked at her with a grin. 'This, my darling, is one movie I can't wait to watch...' and with that, he pulled loose the ties still holding her dress together, so that her beautiful body was revealed to him. 'Thank you,' he whispered, as he lowered his mouth to her flesh, and then, tantalisingly slowly, moved his mouth down her naked body to take his gift...

Want to read more from Honey McGregor?
Choose from Private Pleasures: The Collection and Watch Me Want Me - a novella.

Private Pleasures: The Collection is an anthology of nine erotic fantasies, ranging from playing away to role play, from steamy seductions to total sexual submission...   Great stories, something for your every mood, Honey McGregor's stories are the perfect escape into a world of sexual desire and fulfilment. Close the door, lower the blind, and find pleasure at your fingertips... Private Pleasures is Honey's most popular book - a top bestseller, a top most-wanted, and top most-gifted, book for erotica fans.

Watch Me Want Me oozes fantasy, desire, online temptation, and sexual obsession. But it's also about love. When a young couple stop giving each other the attention they need, they begin to look elsewhere for excitement. Matt seeks his thrills online, watching hot girls, as they play out his requests. But Tanya finds sexual excitement on the other side of the camera, being watched by faceless strangers... Enjoy scenes of slow, sensual, pleasure, in this perfect late night read for women looking for a little extra heat with their bedtime reading

Thank you

Thanks for reading Dina Island, I hope you enjoyed it!
Leave a few words on Amazon if you'd like to share your experience.
You can find me on www.facebook.com/HoneyMcGregorAuthor
You can also visit with me at Honey McGregor's Stories, my personal blog:
www.honeymcgregor.blogspot.com
Until the next time... the pleasure's been all mine... hopefully yours too...

Honey McGregor

Printed in Great Britain
by Amazon

15937959R00031